Copyright © 2005 by Random House, Inc. All rights reserved under International and
Pan-American Copyright Conventions. Published in the United States by Golden Books,
an imprint of Random House Children's Books, a division of Random House, Inc.,
New York, NY 10019, and simultaneously in Canada by Random House of Canada Limited,
Toronto. Golden Books, A Golden Book, A Golden Scratch and Sniff Book, and the G colophon
are registered trademarks of Random House, Inc.
Library of Congress Control Number: 2004112626
ISBN: 978-0-375-83285-7
www.goldenbooks.com
Printed in the United States of America
15 17 19 20 18 16

The Spooky Smells of Halloween

by Mary Man-Kong 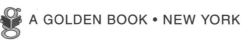 illustrated by Viviana Garofoli

A GOLDEN BOOK • NEW YORK

It's Halloween, and all the children are getting ready.
Sammy is especially excited—he's going to have a Halloween party!
"I can't wait to put on my costume!" Sammy tells his dad.

Sammy's mom sets out a bucket of apples.
"Can I try bobbing for one?" Sammy asks.
"Sure! Give it a test run!" Mom says.

Can you smell the apples?

The whole family decorates the living room—
even Sammy's cat, Buster, helps!

The decorations are almost done—except for one thing.
"Boo!" shouts Sammy.
"That's frightfully fun," Sammy's mom says.

Can you smell the pumpkin?

Sammy puts on his costume for the party.
"Ahoy, mateys!" he cries as he waves his pirate's sword.
Then Sammy gets Buster ready, too.
"You make a great skunk!" Sammy tells his cat.

Sammy's best friend, Katie, is the first to arrive at the party. "I've made a special Halloween punch," says Katie. "It's called berry brew."

Can you smell the Halloween punch?

Now it's party time!
All the guests are busy eating and playing games.

"Everybody have a creepy cookie," Sammy's dad offers.
"They're super spooky!" says Sammy.

Can you smell the Halloween cookies?

"Now it's time to go trick-or-treating!" announces Sammy's mom.
"I hope my bag is big enough," says Sammy.

Sammy, Katie, and all their friends start at Katie's house.
"Trick or treat!" they cry.
"What wonderful costumes!" Katie's mother exclaims.
"Bubble gum for everyone!"

Can you smell the bubble gum?

The children trick-or-treat at all their neighbors' houses.
"I got chocolate, caramel, and candy corn," says Katie.
"I got lollipops, licorice, and lots of taffy," says Sammy.

"What a super Halloween," Sammy says.
"It looks like Buster had a good time, too," adds Katie.
"Wait a minute!" Sammy exclaims. "That isn't Buster!"

Can you smell the skunk?

Happy Halloween!